Deb waves to a girl.
She is Deb's best friend, Meg.
Deb can play at Meg's farm today.

Meg and Deb get eggs from a
flock of hens.
Six fat red hens peck at specks
of grit.

Deb and Meg clip clop on Meg's
black horse, Socks.

Meg and Deb step on the slats of
the pig pen to look at the big hogs.

Deb and Meg swim and get wet.
They trap frogs and let them go.

Deb and Meg rest and smell flowers.
They get snacks from Meg's mom.

Wrens sing.
"I know where a wren's nest is!"
yells Deb.

They read books and write
letters to Meg's Gran.
What a swell farm it is!